Freeing Mr. B & Me

The Sydney Roberts Series–Book 0

Susan Hart Snyder

www.susanhartsnyder.com

Cover design by Micah Kearns
Author photo by Patti Sewall

Freeing Mr. B & Me/ Susan Hart Snyder -- 1st Ed.
ISBN-13: 978-0-9974224-0-5

To Di, because those with whom we travel the longest are the dearest, and because you just can't make this stuff up.

The moment you doubt whether you can fly,
you cease forever to be able to do it.
J.M. BARRIE — *PETER PAN*

CHAPTER ONE

Encased in the darkness of the midnight hour with my computer screen the only light source, I lifted my laptop off my thighs. They had become uncomfortably warm from the hours I had spent burning through Internet sites. Shifting my legs until they stretched across the full length of my couch, I wiggled my toes and turned my neck from side to side. "Where are you, Bobbi Jo?" I asked, lifting my face to the ceiling.

"You'll find her," came an answer, not from the ceiling, but from the hallway behind me. It was my boyfriend Harry. "Because you're too damn fixated on her to give up until you do," he continued as he moved close enough to where I could make out his stubble-covered face and the frustration in his eyes. "And, it's probably gonna kill you, or get you fired when your boss finds you asleep at your desk."

"My boss isn't going to fire me." I straightened up and set the computer on the end table next to me. "You know I couldn't fall asleep during the day. Not even if I tried."

"True, Ms. Queen of the Insomniacs, but you still need to squeeze in a few hours of shut-eye at night if you don't want to add Zombie Queen to your title. Come to bed."

"Not yet. I think I'm really close."

"That's what you thought last night, and the night before that." He crossed his arms. "Where'd this cyber-snoop streak of yours come from, anyway? You used to look down your nose at people who spent all their time glued to their devices."

"I have to find Bobbi Jo, Harry. I thought you understood that. If I don't, I'm never going to have any peace in my life, ever."

"Ever? That's pretty dramatic." Sitting down next to me, he took my hand and enfolded it in his. "You're going to let one low-life woman define the rest of your life? I don't think so."

"Maybe it was too strong a statement, but I can't let that bitch win if I can help it. I can't let her get away with milking my dad for every last dime not telling me about his heart attack for days. Now this." I picked up the statement from the nursing home that was sitting next to the computer and held it up to him. "Bobbi Jo had to have been the one to empty out my Grandma Rose's bank account and the reason why the nursing home bill hasn't been paid. She has no right! She wasn't even on the account! And now they're going to kick Grandma Rose out! Force her into some kind of government-subsidized hellhole!" My voice caught on my last words as I felt the tears start to form in my eyes.

"I know." Harry let go of my hand and put his arm around my shoulder. "But, you're not going to let that happen. You'll be there in a few days and find a good place for her."

"Damn right! It may have to be here in Los Angeles, you know."

"Yeah. We talked about that."

"How am I going to pay for it?"

"We've gone over that too. There are senior advocates that will help you figure it all out."

"Yeah, yeah, I know. I'm repeating myself. I'm sorry," I sighed.

"So, turn the computer off, will ya. Let's go to bed." Harry grabbed my hand again and squeezed it.

"I'll be there in a few minutes. I really think I've found a lead."

"All right. I know better than to try to talk you out of it. If you're not in bed in thirty minutes I'm coming back out here and carrying you there."

"Now that could be fun." I smiled at him.

"It could be." He shrugged his shoulders. "If we didn't have to be up in less than six hours."

"Yes, work." I turned to grab my laptop. Good old practical Harry. Spontaneity was not his strong suit.

Returning to the site that was already up on the computer, I typed in the name of Bobbi Jo's former head cook at her restaurant. Sure enough, up popped his picture. "Javier Garcia! Got ya!" There was no doubt in my mind he would know where she was. There was even half a chance they might be living together. You'd have to be totally naive not to think that the two of them were having an affair when they were working together. And, my dad was just that. Although from the sadness that had settled in his eyes the last time I saw him, he must have figured out how devastating a mistake he made in marrying Bobbi Jo–for both of us.

CHAPTER TWO

After living with cancer for seven years, my mother passed away when I was in college. She was far too young and so full of life. It was very hard. She was the type who volunteered to coach our soccer team because no one else would do it, despite never having played herself.

My dad was crazy about her. He held it together for her during all those years she received treatment. I ended up with a lot of the household responsibilities because he was no cook and definitely not a housekeeper. After she died he pulled into himself for a long time. He ate alone at nearby restaurants and watched sports at the local bars. He never once ventured into his shop to start a new project.

Then along came Bobbi Jo.

My Grandma Rose had moved three blocks from us after my grandpa died and was part of our lives from the time I was very young. With my mom an only child like me, we were the only family my grandmother had in California. A few years after my mother passed away, Grandma Rose fell and broke her hip and my dad hired Bobbi Jo–Texas belle, professional caregiver, and practiced gold digger–to help out.

It didn't take Bobbi Jo long to size up the situation, and work it *and my dad* to her advantage. I was happy for him at first. Actually, I was relieved. By then I was well into my own life and it took the burden of worrying about him off me.

When I went home and discovered that Bobbi Jo had completely redecorated my mom's house in the neo-tacky style, I felt a tiny stir of foreboding, but I was too busy to pay much attention to it. I didn't even venture into my old room to see what may have changed there. Big mistake.

When Bobbi Jo convinced my dad to move back to her hometown of El Paso, Texas, the nagging suspicion became a little more pronounced. But, I still wasn't all that worried.

Then they sent for Grandma Rose and promptly put her in a nursing home in an El Paso suburb. Shortly after that, my dad bought Bobbi Jo a fancy house, a motorhome, and that white Cadillac she had always wanted. He also bought her a restaurant she ran into the ground in less than a year. And finally, the foreboding I ignored for so long roared to life. But, it was too late.

It was six days before Bobbi Jo bothered to call and tell me my father had suffered a massive heart attack. When I flew back to see him the first time, he was still in the hospital, but his prognosis was pretty good. On my second visit, he was home, and Bobbi Jo was taking care of him by feeding him pork chops fried in six inches of oil and smothered in gravy. She even encouraged him to light up a cigarette with her to go along with their cocktails.

She wanted him dead. And, she got her wish.

She called me right away when he had his second heart attack, but he didn't survive that one.

Attending the pathetic memorial service Bobbi Jo had for him was one of the saddest times of my life. I was so numb I asked nothing about his estate or belongings. I did want his ashes, or at least part of them, to sprinkle over my mother's grave, but Bobbi Jo would have none of it. They were already enshrined in a cheap urn sitting atop her garish mantel.

When I dropped in on Grandma Rose that trip, I decided not to take her to the memorial. She was well into dementia at that point, and only had fleeting moments where I think she knew who I was. Before I left I debated whether to leave her in El Paso or take her back to Los Angeles. I concluded that so long as they were doing a good job where she was, the move would probably be too traumatic. Bobbi Jo reassured me she would take good care of Grandma Rose and check on her at least once a week. Why I believed that, I don't know.

Then the bills started coming to my apartment, one after the next—nursing home, medical, credit cards ...

Then Bobbi Jo disappeared.

And I had been looking for her ever since.

I managed to unravel most of the web Bobbi Jo had tangled me in with no financial repercussions or damage to my credit. However, there was still the issue of Grandma Rose. I didn't have the means to take care of her. I also didn't want her to end up in some sad facility in a city that had never really been her home.

When I received the latest letter from the nursing home, I knew I had to go. I decided to drive as I'd have to sell a kidney to pay for the outrageous cost of a last-minute airline ticket. And there was a good chance I'd be driving Grandma Rose back with me.

There was no way I was going to spend any time in El Paso without tracking down Bobbi Jo and confronting her. I knew there was no chance of getting my father's and grandmother's money back, but Bobbi Jo was also in possession of all my childhood mementos. Or, at least I hoped she still was. Somehow when she and my father moved to Texas, they managed to take with them all of the family photos, any representation of the life I had shared with my parents. And, I was going to get them back.

CHAPTER THREE

I spent most of the eight hundred miles to El Paso rehearsing what I was going to say to Bobbi Jo, matching my speed with my anger. Fortunately, the other trucks and cars on the Interstate had their own motivation for ignoring the speed limit, and the highway patrol left us alone.

It was early evening when I pulled into the parking lot of Grandma Rose's nursing home but the sun was still bright and hot. My God, it was hot! June in Los Angeles is often overcast but not in El Paso.

As I opened the car door, the wind almost ripped it off its hinges. Holding my sundress down in order to keep my brand of underwear to myself, I waded through the gusts to the entrance, with my curly hair whisked into a tangled mass that doubled the size of my head. Despite the heat there was no danger of sweaty armpits. Perspiration dried up the second it hit your skin.

Looking at brown mountains stacked up in the distance, I wondered how people actually lived there? Poor things.

After stopping in at the reception desk and making an appointment with the administrator for the next morning to talk about moving Grandma Rose, I made my way down the corridor to her room. The place wasn't dirty but it didn't matter. It still smelled of urine and decay. And, no matter how much all-purpose cleaner they used, they couldn't cover it up. It almost made the smell worse.

I remember walking down a similar corridor with Grandma Rose when we visited an old friend of hers. She turned to me and said, "If you ever have to put me in one of these places, just shoot me first!" And, here she was.

She was in a two-bed room, and her roommate was asleep in the far bed, lying face up. It startled me at first because her skin was so gray and her eyes so sunken I thought she might be dead. No. She was breathing, but it was loud and labored. That couldn't be good.

Turning to Grandma Rose, she was also lying on her back, but her eyes were open.

"Hey there, Grandma." I gently touched her shoulder. "It's Sydney."

"I have a prolapsed bladder." She rested her cloudy eyes on me.

"I'm sorry to hear that."

"I need to pee."

"Oh, okay. Shall I get the nurse?"

"You're the nurse," she said in an accusing tone. "You're supposed to do it."

"No. I'm Sydney, Grandma. Your granddaughter."

"What did you do with the nurse?" She patted her sheet with her palm until she found the control for the bed. Pushing a button she lifted the head of it until she was sitting straight up.

"Nothing. She's right down the hall." I reached out to touch her hand.

Jerking it away she let go of the remote and grabbed the call button for the nurse's station. "You can't get away with this!" She pressed her thumb down hard on the red button.

"Grandma, you don't have to keep pushing the button," I said quietly. "I'm sure the nurse heard your call. She'll be right here." I reached out once again and put my hand over hers.

Slapping it with her free hand, she cried out, "No! Don't hurt me! Help! Help! She kidnapped the nurse!"

Oh boy. Keeping my voice low and calm, I said, "Grandma, it's okay. It's Sydney. Remember? I used to spend the night at your house. You taught me how to play gin rummy. I'm here for you."

Her eyes scanned my face. "Gin rummy?"

"Yes. We'd play for hours while we watched professional bowling tournaments on TV." I never really understood her whole bowling fascination. It's about as exciting as watching paint dry.

The nurse finally entered the room. "What is it, Rose?"

"I have a prolapsed bladder."

"Yes. I know." She straightened the blankets at the bottom of the bed.

"I need to pee."

"I just took you fifteen minutes ago."

"I need to pee," Grandma Rose said again.

"Okay then. I'll send someone else in to help you. I need to finish my paperwork."

"She can do it." She pointed at me. "She's a nurse."

The nurse looked at me.

Darn. This was a whole other level of care that I hadn't taken into consideration. However, if I was going to drive

Grandma Rose back to Los Angeles with me, and even have her stay until I settled her elsewhere, I had better get used to it. "Okay. I'll help you. Just give me a minute."

Motioning to the nurse to follow me into the corridor, I moved away from the door so Grandma Rose couldn't hear me. "I'm Sydney, her granddaughter. You were here the last time I visited, right?"

"Yes." The nurse looked down at her watch.

"Her dementia seems to have worsened quite a bit since my last visit."

"That's typical." She looked over at the nurse's station.

Becoming peeved at the woman's obvious desire to rush away, I said, "What's your name?"

"Margarite."

"I'd appreciate a quick rundown of her behaviors so I can know how to respond, Margarite."

"If you want a thorough consult, you'll need to take that up with her doctor."

"Just give me the short version, Margarite." I folded my arms. "I'm not going to be here that long."

"Fine." She looked at her watch again. "She's been pretty paranoid of late. Thinks everyone's out to get her. It's more pronounced at night. She's even gotten physically aggressive at times."

"My sweet little grandma?"

"It happens. Dementia manifests in a lot of different ways. Violence is not uncommon." Margarite tugged on the waist of her elastic uniform pants.

"How should I handle it?"

"Just keep a calm demeanor. The episodes don't last. She's on meds. They help."

"In what way?" I asked, thinking they didn't seem to be doing any good.

"They've had success in some patients by slowing the progress of dementia, and sedatives definitely help."

"Sedatives?"

"Right."

"You knock them out?"

"Calm them down. I have to go now. My shift is almost over and I haven't finished my reports."

"Fine then. Thanks for your help," I said to her retreating back.

I managed to get Grandma Rose to the bathroom and back twice during my visit without having her think I had kidnapped a nurse. Taking her on was going to be a lot more challenging than I thought, but I owed it to her to get her out of El Paso and back to Los Angeles. Despite having to watch her own daughter whither away, she had been a rock for me during my mother's illness. I needed to be there for her. I just hoped the meeting with the nursing home administrator would go smoothly, and he wouldn't think I was there to settle any debts, because that was just not going to happen.

CHAPTER FOUR

Leaving the nursing home with dusk just beginning to set in, I double-checked the map app on my phone to make sure I knew the exact location of the house where Javier told me Bobbi Jo resided. It had been a long day, but I was thriving on adrenaline. I had no intention of waiting until the morning to call on Miss Bobbi Jo. I thought I might have a better chance of catching her in the evening.

When I talked to Javier, he'd revealed that he and Bobbi Jo were no longer lovers, or even friends. Turns out she duped him the way she had the rest of us. He was more than happy to give me her address when he found out the purpose of my visit. He had even given me her phone number, but I didn't want to call and allow her the chance to squirm her way out of seeing me.

When I made my first pass by her house I was surprised to find it was nothing like the ridiculous colonial my father had bought her. That thing was so out of place in West Texas. This house fit a whole lot better, with its stucco siding, flat roof, and rod iron bars on all the windows. I wondered whether those bars were to keep the bad guys in or out.

On closer inspection, the place was not only nothing like her previous house in style, it was also nothing like it in worth. The flat roof was sagging, the stucco was chipped, and the front yard was a scorched plot of sad plants and lava-colored rocks. She was apparently between sugar daddies.

Making a U-turn and stopping my car in front of the neighbor's house two doors down from hers, I stepped out and clicked the lock–twice. Bobbi Jo's was not the only sorry house on the block.

Walking across her yard rather than up the front path, I hoped to avoid being spotted. There was a very good chance she wouldn't come to the door if she knew I was the one standing there. As I knocked, I looked over at the white Cadillac in the driveway. It was brown with dust and dotted with rusting dents. I was glad my dad didn't have to see it like that. He always kept his cars in pristine condition. The good thing was that it was an indication she was home.

Knocking louder the second time, I heard several low woofs coming from inside, followed by footsteps. Finally, the door opened, and there she was–in short shorts and a crop top, neither of which did anything to hide her puffy dimpled skin. A lit cigarette dangled from her fingers. She was surrounded by a pack of dogs in various shapes and sizes, and before she looked at me she whacked them with her foot, and yelled, "Get out of here! Get! Now!"

Turning her attention on me, her eyes reflected suspicion before recognition.

"Hello, Bobbi Jo." I put my foot on the threshold in case she had any ideas about slamming the door in my face.

"Sydney," she said in her phony Texas drawl. "Howdy. Good to see you, honey. What brings you here?"

Good to see me? Like we were friends? Like she hadn't disappeared out of my life, leaving disaster in her wake?

"My grandmother, for starters, and the matter of her being kicked out of the nursing home for non-payment." I thought about easing into the conversation, but she had already stoked the fires of my anger, and there was no putting it out now.

"Kicked out? They can't do that."

"Of course they can. And, they're going to. My grandmother had plenty of money to cover the cost of her care, Bobbi Jo. What happened to it?"

"I don't know, honey. Your daddy handled all the money." She took a long drag on her cigarette, then reached past me and flicked the ashes onto the porch. Classy.

Staring hard at her, I took a breath, trying to slow my heartbeat. I had been planning this conversation for a very long time, and I wanted to be very clear with her about what she had done to us. "No, Bobbi Jo. *You* handled the money, *and my father.* You spent it all, and left us with nothing, and apparently yourself with nothing either!" I gestured toward her front yard. "You told me you were going to take care of Grandma Rose, Bobbi Jo. You didn't! When was the last time you even saw her?"

"I visit her every week, just like I promised. I love your granny. I had no idea they were kicking her out."

Oh my God. What a liar! "How could you not have known, Bobbi Jo? You talked my dad into selling her house and bringing her out here. There was an account set up to fund all her expenses, and there is nothing left in it. What happened to it, Bobbi Jo?"

"Nursing homes are very expensive, Sydney, several thousand dollars a month."

"And, she had plenty to cover it. You ran through my father's money, and when it was all gone, you moved onto Grandma Rose's! You drove an old lady to homelessness. How can you live with yourself?"

"That was very hurtful, Sydney. I was good to your daddy and granny." Bobbi Jo turned her back on me and reached for a dish on a table in her entry.

Oh, brother. Was it possible she believed she had done no wrong? My choice was to stand there and continue to try and badger her into taking some responsibility for ruining the last years of my father's and grandmother's lives, or to get what I came for and never think about her again.

The woman was never going to admit her own guilt, and there were things I wanted from her, so I said, "Okay, Bobbi Jo, whatever."

As I watched her stub her cigarette out in the dish, I noticed the urn next to it. It was the one that held my father's ashes, and one of the things I had driven eight hundred miles to get. I wasn't going to ask for it first, because she had already turned me down once. I waited for her attention to return to me, and said, "When I visited you and my father the last time, I noticed there was a box of my things, photo albums and yearbooks, in the guest bedroom closet. Do you still have it?"

"Hmm." She put her finger on her chin. "I'm not sure if that box made the move or not."

"Would you mind checking? It's the only trace of my childhood I have left."

"It may be in the garage out back. You can set yourself down there while I have a look." She nodded at the filthy white plastic lawn chair on the porch. When I stepped back from the threshold, she closed the door.

I guess I wasn't being invited in.

Looking down at the chair, there was no way I was using it. Holding my hair up off my neck, I fanned my face. Night was setting in soon, and it was still way too hot. Turning back to the door, it took me only a split second to decide to let myself into the house. I wanted to see if she had anything else of my father's or grandmother's that I wanted. With her search taking her to the garage, Bobbi Jo would be a few minutes before she returned.

Trying the door handle, it was locked, but as I pushed on it, the door opened. Bobbi Jo hadn't shut it all the way. Hurrying in, I left the door open behind me. As I walked into the family room, a long-eared low-slung dog trotted up to greet me. I wasn't that up on dog breeds, but I was pretty sure he was a Basset Hound. There were no other dogs with him, so I assumed they had followed Bobbi Jo outside. "Hi boy," I whispered and patted the top of his head, wanting to make friends so he wouldn't out me to Bobbi Jo by barking. He didn't seem all that interested in protecting his turf, staring up at me with bloodshot eyes as his tongue sprinkled drool on the worn carpet.

Looking around, I immediately spotted my grandad's oak rocker. My grandmother told me she was going to leave it to me in her will. It held great memories for me of my grandad holding court from that chair in his bungalow in Hollywood. His was the only home left on his block, as the rest had succumbed to apartment development decades before. Grandad told great stories from that chair, stories that were so vivid and magical it made me want to be a writer. For practical reasons, I wasn't making my living as a writer yet–I was working as an editor–but I was determined. And that rocker was both a reminder of where I came from and where I was headed. I wanted it.

I didn't recognize anything else in the living room or kitchen as having belonged to my parents, pre-Bobbi Jo. She had pretty much thrown out every trace of my mother when she redecorated our Los Angeles home. It was just going to be my dad's ashes and the rocker that I asked for. How could she say no to that?

Hurrying back to the porch with the dog at my heels, I gave him a gentle push back into the house. When he tried to follow me outside I closed the door.

Bobbi Jo had been gone so long I wondered if she had forgotten me or perhaps hoped I'd disappear. When the door finally opened, she held a box in her arms.

"There you go." She handed it to me.

The cardboard was so soft it felt like the box was going to collapse, and it smelled of mold. Looking down into it I could see watermarks on the scrapbook that was on top. Great. I'd be lucky if there was one decent photograph of my parents and myself. "This box is ruined." I held it as far from my nose as I could.

"You're lucky I still had it." She pulled a cigarette from a small pocket on the front of her shirt. Handy. "You could've taken your things any time you wanted, you know, if you'd bothered to pack up your own room."

Studying her lined face, which was several Botox appointments shy of the wrinkle-free look she used to go for, I thought about telling Bobbi Jo why it was so difficult to spend any time in my mother's house with *her* in it, but I would have been wasting my breath. If I was going to get the rocker and the ashes, I needed to play nice.

"You're right." I tossed an olive branch at her. "So, what have you been up to? Are you still in the restaurant business?"

"I'm doing interior design now." She lit the cigarette with a lighter she had taken from the front pocket of her shorts. I wondered what else she had stuffed into her wardrobe. I wouldn't have been surprised to see her pull a flask of whiskey out of her sizeable bra.

"You always did enjoy decorating." What did she call her business, Tacky by Bobbi?

"Yes, I did. And, my friends begged me for a long time to help them out with design, so I thought, why not?"

"Why not?" I pressed my lips into a grin, hoping I didn't come off as too fake. "By the way, do you still have that oak rocker that belonged to my grandad? My grandmother promised it to me, and it certainly isn't your style."

"Yeah, it's still here. Your father insisted on keeping it."

"I'd like to have it."

"No."

"No? Why not?"

"Because he left me his things, and I'm keeping them."

"That rocker was not one of *his* things. It belongs to my grandmother. Besides, you have plenty of his things, plus all that he bought for you, the jewelry, the Cadillac sitting in your driveway. I want the rocker, Bobbi Jo. That, and I would like some of his ashes."

"No." She put her hand on the doorknob. When she did, the Basset Hound, who had been sitting at her feet listening to our conversation, started to trot out onto the porch. Bending down and yanking his chain, she pulled his front feet off the ground and dragged him back in. "Get back in here!" she commanded. "Now, scoot!" She shoved his haunches with her foot, and he yelped.

"You hurt him!"

"It's time you leave!" She straightened up and pushed the door. "You got what you wanted. Go! And, don't ever bother coming around here again pretending like you care a whit about me!"

"Like you care about me or my grandmother!" I yelled at the closing door. "You're one nasty human being, Bobbi Jo, and in what little time you have left of your debauched life, I hope that you get all that you deserve!"

Staring at the door with my heart pounding, I was so frustrated. Dammit! She was not going to win this one!

I was coming back for that rocker and those ashes, even if I had to break into the house to get them!

CHAPTER FIVE

That night, after I put my small suitcase onto the luggage rack in the motel room, I pulled the flowered bedspread off, set it on a side chair and washed my hands. I'm not normally a germaphobe, but there's something about motel rooms. It's probably the warnings about the microscopic critters and insects that infamously reside in them, because the thought of sitting on a motel bedspread gives me the heebie-jeebies.

Spreading a newspaper over the blanket, I set the box Bobbi Jo gave me down on it and placed the new plastic bin I had purchased next to it.

One by one, I began to sort through the soggy pages of my youth. My high school yearbooks were almost unreadable, the messages that my friends wrote in the margins a blur. Those years had been a blur themselves anyway, with my mother's cancer diagnosis coming when I was a freshman.

Next, I pulled out a scrapbook I had put together of our trip to New York City to visit my dad's brother and his family, and to see the requisite sites. The postcard from the Empire State Building had survived, along with a photo of my mom, dad, and me taken by another tourist on the ferry to the Statue of Liberty. I planned to have that photo restored. It may have been the last best time we had together as a family.

The baby pictures and elementary school photos I found in random envelopes were pretty moldy, but I could probably have something done with those also. I guess my childhood memories weren't a total loss.

Stacking the things neatly back in the plastic bin, I lifted it up and felt its weight. It wasn't very heavy. So, that was it– my entire youth in one box. No parents. No family homes. Just a handful of relatives in the Bronx, and a grandma in a nursing home in El Paso, Texas, a grandma who needed to get out of that nursing home pronto.

But, that was tomorrow. For tonight I planned to drown my sorrows in fast food, and to plot a burglary.

The next morning, after listening to my Grandma Rose's options offered by the nursing home administrator, I was grateful that my father had designated me to have power of attorney for her. Otherwise, I may have been forced to take the man's suggestion and hand her over to a state facility–that, or kidnap her. And since I was already planning to burglarize Bobbi Jo's place later that day, I didn't really need a kidnapping offense to go along with a burglary charge.

I was surprised when the administrator said I could pick Grandma Rose up as early as that afternoon, but then, they weren't making any money by having her take up a bed without payment. Knowing I wanted to get out of El Paso as soon as possible, and already committed to bringing her to Los Angeles, I decided that this afternoon would do just fine. She didn't have many belongings, so it wasn't going to take much time to have her out of there.

When the meeting was through, I stopped in at Grandma Rose's room to see what I would need to bring back with me to pack her clothes and personal items. Sadly, for someone who once owned a large home, a couple of file boxes were all that was necessary.

On my way to pick up the boxes, I decided to drive by Bobbi Jo's house to see if she was home. My plan was to go back and forth between her street and the nearby shopping center until the Cadillac disappeared from the driveway. With the Texas heat, there was no way I was going to roast in my car while staking out her place. Not only that, I didn't want to arouse suspicion in the neighbors.

On my first pass by her house, Bobbi Jo's car was still in the driveway. When I returned the second time after a stop at a smoothie shop, she appeared from around the back of the house, stopping to open the metal gate with her purse in the crook of her arm and cigarette between her lips. Yay!

Ducking down, I accelerated, driving the full length of her street and around the corner. Pulling over, I waited ten minutes then headed back to her house. She was gone. Now what? Thinking I should hurry, in the event that Bobbi Jo was only out for a quick booze run, I pulled my car up the driveway and under the window without bars I had noticed the day before. I hoped my car would at least partially block anyone passing by from seeing me break in.

Break in! What was I thinking? My heart pounded as I climbed onto the hood of the car and squatted down. Putting both palms on the window, I tried sliding it open. No luck. But, I had come prepared. My father had insisted I keep a full emergency kit in my car at all times, and in it was a screwdriver. Wedging it into the small space between the window and the frame, I pushed on it and jiggled it back and forth. Sure enough, the window moved.

Checking the street to make sure no one was watching, I pushed it open all the way and removed the warped screen that was barely attached. Dropping the screen gently to the floor, I put one leg through the window, squeezed the other leg through, and landed in the small breakfast nook adjacent to the kitchen. Then, I closed the window and set the screen back in.

Rushing to the entryway, I grabbed the plastic bag I had stuffed into the pocket of my jeans. Opening the urn with my father's ashes, I carefully dumped them into the bag and knotted the top. Picking up the dish that I had seen Bobbi Jo use as an ashtray the day before, I poured its contents into the empty urn and ran and grabbed a couple more ashtrays from the family room. I poured those ashes and butts in also. That was so much fun! I doubted she'd ever bother to open the urn, but if she did–surprise!

Tucking my shirt into my jeans, I unbuttoned it, slid the bag with my dad's ashes down it, buttoned it back up and trotted to the family room. Grabbing the rocker, I dragged it through the kitchen to the back door. When I opened it, I was greeted by Bobbi Jo's canine pack. Uh oh! I shut the door. Quickly searching her cupboards until I found a bag of dog food, I opened the door, tossed out two handfuls and dragged the rocker through, making sure the door locked behind me.

The kibble didn't occupy the dogs for long, but at least I had made friends. None came after me with bared teeth. Opening the metal gate that led to the driveway, I used the rocker and my legs to block the dogs from their escape route.

I managed to get through without having any of them follow me.

As I turned around to make sure the gate was secure, I noticed the Bassett Hound caught in plastic netting that was atop a low pile of rubbish at the back of the yard. He wasn't fussing at all, just sitting there in the blazing sun and looking at me with those sad eyes, his long tongue dangling almost to his feet.

Jeez! Poor guy! How long had he been like that? He probably hadn't had any water for hours. Bobbi Jo had just walked by him and left him like that. She had to have seen him. Why did people like her even have dogs? It wasn't like she cared about them.

Sighing, I looked to the street. Still quiet. Lifting the rocker and walking as fast as I could, I set it down, opened the trunk and placed it in there. I'd known it wasn't going to fit, so I'd bought bungee cords to hold my trunk lid shut. My dad had taught me that also. "Thank you, Dad," I said as I pulled the ashes from my shirt, opened the passenger door, and put them in the glove compartment. "Sorry about this." I patted the bag of ashes before I shut the compartment. "I'll find you a proper home. I promise." Weird, I know, but somehow comforting.

Running back through the gate, I rushed over to the hound and held my hand out. I wasn't sure if he was hurt, and knew there was a chance he could lash out at me. Although, really? Running my hand over the knot on the top of his head while he stared up at me with complete trust, I doubted that dog would ever lash out at anyone.

"Let me take a look, boy." I lifted his back foot. One by one I released his paws, and he was soon free. Looking around I finally spotted a hose bib and some empty bowls beside it. Filling all of them I made sure the hound got his share before the other dogs pushed him aside.

"Your owner should be reported to PETA, guys," I said to the pack. "But, I don't have time to take care of that right now."

Hurrying across the yard, I heard the jingle of a chain right behind me. When I stopped to open the gate, I felt a hot wet breath on my calves. Looking down, there was the Bassett Hound staring up at me expectantly.

"No. No. No. You can't come, buddy."

He just sat there and raised his eyebrows at me–really–one at a time. Then, he woofed a low woof and looked at me with those huge hopeful brown eyes.

And, what was I supposed to do? Leave him behind? To be abused by Bobbi Jo?

Nope. I didn't have it in me. So, I dognapped. I burglarized, and I dognapped.

Looking through my rearview mirror at the hound in my backseat and the raised trunk lid holding down the stolen rocker, I started to back down the driveway, when I caught a glimpse of white behind me. Uh oh! It was Bobbi Jo! What to do? What to do?

Deciding to take the offense, I killed the engine, stepped out of my car, and walked toward Bobbi Jo as she marched up her driveway.

"Why are you here?" she asked, stopping in front of me and jabbing her fists into her hips. Before I could respond, her attention was drawn to the rocker sticking out of my trunk, and she shrieked, "Thief! You broke into my house! I'm calling the police!" Just then, the hound decided to pop up to see what all the fuss was about. When Bobbi Jo caught sight of him watching us from my rear window, she turned on me, her eyes spitting fire. "And you stole my dog, too?" Rushing back to her car, she reached in through the open driver's door and pulled out her purse.

I hurried toward her while watching her dig for her cellphone. "You were abusing that dog! If I hadn't come along, he would have died of heat stroke with the rest of them!" I looked up at the dogs that had trotted over and were lined up at the back gate, as interested in the action as the hound. At least they weren't barking. We didn't need the neighbors involved.

"I do not abuse my dogs! I rescued every one of them!" She jutted her phone at me and started to dial it.

"You're not calling the police, Bobbi Jo." I reached out to stop her.

She slapped my hand away before I could grab the phone. "Don't touch me, you evil little witch! I knew it would come to this someday! I warned your daddy about you a long time ago. That sweet little daughter act of yours was all pretend! You just wanted his money!"

That did it! I wrenched the phone from her hand and chucked it across the yard. "His money? Oh my God, Bobbi Jo! His money? You're getting me confused with yourself!" I yelled to her back, as she ran across her yard to retrieve the phone, as fast as her jiggly little body could move.

On her heels, I continued, "You're the thief! Not me! You used that fat ass and those big boobs of yours to reel my father in, then you drove him to his death!"

When she reached the phone, she bent over to pick it up, and shook it next to her ear, like she was testing it for rattles. What an idiot! She started to dial again.

"No! You call the police, Bobbi Jo, and I'm going straight to an attorney to file a criminal suit against you for stealing my grandmother's savings! I swear; I will use every last dime I have to take you down! You had no legal authority to take the funds from my grandmother's account, and you know it! My father and I were the only ones with power of attorney for my grandmother. You had to have faked my signature to get that money, and I'm going to prove it! Then, we'll see who spends more time in prison, you or me!"

Holding her finger over the phone, she whined, "You broke into my house! The police are going to be a whole lot more interested in that than your granny's bank account!"

"It was unlocked," I lied. "And, that's *my* rocker." I looked over at my car.

"But, it's not your dog!"

"Like you care about that dog! You let it fry in this heat, all tangled up in your garbage heap! You don't want it!"

Focusing her eyes on her phone and puckering her lined mouth, she finally said, "I'm not going to let you get away with robbing me," and started to dial again.

"Okay, Bobbi Jo, you make that call, and I'll make mine to my attorney. But, keep in mind that there are records of every withdrawal from Grandma Rose's account, and there are handwriting experts who will prove that your signature is on what I expect is quite a few of them."

Still standing with her hand poised over the phone, Bobbi Jo hesitated. She was having doubts. I had her! "I'm leaving now, Bobbi Jo, with the rocker and the dog. Don't test me on this," I warned her, keeping up the pressure. Pointedly looking over at her sad little house, I continued, "You don't have the money to spend on attorneys."

"Isn't that just like you to prey on a poor defenseless woman who has fallen on hard times."

Oh, brother. Of course she was going to play the victim. "You're anything but defenseless, Bobbi Jo. And, I have no doubt in my mind that you already have your next sugar daddy in your sights." Poor guy!

"You better watch yourself! I still have a mind to call the police!" She stuck the phone in my face.

"You won't," I bluffed, not really trusting that I was right.

"You were always such a brat!" She dropped her hand to her side and raised her chin up at me. "I'm going to let you go for now. But, I'd watch your back, if I were you. I could change my mind any time and let the rest of the world know what a little crook you are!"

"You better watch *your back* too! You never know when I might change *my* mind!" Staring her down, I decided that was enough. She was going to remain forever delusional about her own true nature. I just had to hope she had enough sense to take my threat seriously, and not follow up on hers. "Just move your car, so I can get out of here," was all I said.

Huffing, she turned on her heel and stomped over to her car.

Checking my rearview mirror, I followed Bobbi Jo's car down her driveway and on to the street. My adrenaline was still pumping from our fight and from the fear that she wouldn't keep that big mouth of hers shut about my felonious exploits. I needed to get Grandma Rose and the rest of us out of Texas, fast!

CHAPTER SIX

"I have a prolapsed bladder." It was Grandma Rose for the thousandth time, and we had barely crossed the border into Arizona. "I have a prolapsed bladder," she repeated. "I have to pee."

It was going to be a long ride–but at least Texas was behind us, and I could stop checking my rearview mirror every few minutes for a cop car. Or could I? Could I be arrested in Arizona or California for a crime I committed in Texas? I had no idea, which meant I was probably going to spend the rest of the ride worrying about it.

"Are you sure you need to pee?" I asked. "We stopped ten minutes ago at that gas station. Do you remember?" I looked over at her, sitting with her hands folded in her lap, staring straight ahead. She looked so small. Childlike really. But, boy could she yell–and fight.

When the aide at the nursing home helped her out of the wheelchair and started leading her to my car, Grandma Rose slapped at her, and shouted, "Help! Help! I'm being kidnapped!"

It took a lot of cajoling and the promise of a strawberry milk shake before we finally settled her into the car.

And, then it started.

"I have a prolapsed bladder. I have to pee."

"Okay." I didn't want to risk putting it off. I hadn't been with her enough to know when her threats to pee her pants were real. "I'll stop at the next off-ramp with a fast food restaurant. You can pee there. We can get something to eat then, too. Maybe they'll have strawberry milk shakes."

The whole stopping thing took a major battle plan, with the Bassett Hound to consider as well as Grandma Rose. During the ride, the dog was pretty content in the back seat surrounded by our boxes, so long as he could keep his nose aimed at the air conditioning fan. That meant he spent the entire ride drooling on the console.

For the time being I was using a bungee cord for the dog's leash and my Grandma Rose's bedpan from her nursing home room for a water bowl. I had also stuffed a large wad of plastic bags into my purse to use when the hound did his business. So, that was all good. The problem was what to do with him when I took my grandmother to the bathroom.

The only solution I could come up with was to find a spot of shade to park the car, and to leave the windows open. Then I'd get Grandma Rose to the bathroom as quickly as I could encourage her to move, while praying no one stole my car or my stuff while I was gone. I couldn't really count on the Bassett Hound to keep thieves at bay. He'd probably just lick them to death.

As I was walking Grandma Rose back to the car from the fast food restaurant bathroom, she said, "I'm hungry! Why won't you feed me? Where's my milk shake?" in a voice loud enough to have the heads of everyone in the parking lot turn in our direction.

"We're going to order our food at the drive-through window, Grandma. I don't want to leave the dog in the hot car any longer."

"I need to eat!" she shouted. "You're torturing me!"

"Let me get you into the car. There's not a long line. We'll have our food in a few minutes." I pushed her along with the hand I had draped around her back.

"You're hurting me!" She shifted, trying to shake my arm off her.

"I'm just trying to help you into the car." I opened the passenger door and nudged her toward the seat.

"Help! Help! I'm being kidnapped!" she yelled, standing rooted to the asphalt.

"Is everything all right?" I heard a voice ask.

When I looked behind me, a policeman was standing there. Holy shit! My brain kicked into B movie crime drama mode. Had Bobbi Jo changed her mind? Did he know about my Texas crime spree? Had he run my license numbers? Was there an APB out on me? Ridiculous. He couldn't know who I was. He was just trying to find out about Grandma Rose. But, my hands were shaking anyway.

In a pitch, much higher than my normal voice, I said, "It's okay, officer," and tapped my finger to my head. "Dementia."

Stepping around me until he had a clear view of Grandma Rose," he asked, "Are you okay, ma'am?" As if he actually thought I might be hurting her. Oh boy! Maybe he did suspect something about me. No! No! No! Just stay calm.

"Get away from me, you!" Grandma Rose spat at him.

Recoiling, he stepped back.

I turned a palm up at him in an *I told you so* gesture.

Stiffening his back and adjusting his service belt to cover for his reaction to Grandma Rose, the officer said, "Best of luck, ma'am."

"Thank you." I turned my back to him, busying myself with Grandma Rose. I wanted him gone.

He was very helpful in one respect, and that was to make him the enemy rather than me. Grandma Rose was suddenly very cooperative about getting into the car.

She was even happier when I handed her a strawberry milkshake. She sucked on that straw for a hundred miles–a hundred miles with nary a mention of a prolapsed bladder.

It gave me time to call Harry and check in about the assisted living facility I had found through a senior advocacy center right before I left for El Paso. They had a room for Grandma Rose! Thank goodness! I loved the woman, but the last few hours convinced me that I was not prepared in any way to have her live with us.

Harry also told me that the advocacy center was helping line up doctors to help with her health issues. She had several of them, the most serious being her heart. The medical reports the nursing home had sent along indicated that Grandma Rose's heart was giving out. I would need to deal with that when I got back to L.A.

Driving into the sunset, I considered stopping for the night because we would not make Los Angeles until the morning. I quickly changed my mind, though, when I noticed that Grandma Rose had nodded off and the Bassett Hound had settled down for a long nap in the back seat.

No. The easiest thing to do was to keep driving. I'd just turn the radio on real low, enjoy the quiet, and try to figure out what in the hell I was going to do with a big dog in our small apartment–and how I was going to explain him to Harry, not to mention my cat Alice. If I knew Alice, she was not going to be a happy camper.

Oh, and there was the matter of thinking up a name for him. He had no tags dangling from the chain around his neck, so I had no idea what Bobbi Jo called him, if anything. I probably wouldn't have used it anyway. He deserved a fresh start just as much as the rest of us. Checking him out in the rearview mirror, flopped down on his side, I smiled. He was just one of those animals that did that for you.

As my eyes shifted from the hound to the box of my childhood memories on the seat next to him, my smile faded. Pulling my eyes away from it and back to the road, I exhaled. I certainly didn't have much to show for my childhood, or the rest of my thirty-plus years, even. Having little physical representation of proof of my existence shouldn't have mattered much. I was never much of a *thing* person anyway. I never understood women who wanted someone else's initials on their purses, in large, gold pot-metal letters no less.

But, what evidence had I acquired that I had contributed anything at all to the greater good? A few well-edited manuscripts? A four-year relationship with a nice guy that hadn't moved beyond the boyfriend stage? An urban tribe with a taste for IPA, sushi, and farcical humor served up with chives and onions?

What happened to those grand plans for changing the world with a mighty pen? What happened to the dreams of venturing into lands where others feared to tread? To challenging the evil and the misguided? To protecting the young and the defenseless? I sighed again.

Had I lost my nerve? Or, had my life become too comfortable?

A little bit of both probably. But, I was far too young to be lulled to sleep in a Barcalounger. "Time to wake up, woman!" I said out loud, slapping the steering wheel.

Grandma Rose stirred, and I looked over, hoping I hadn't awakened her prolapsed bladder. When she settled down again, I reached out and patted her arm.

"It's going to be all right," I whispered to her, then glanced in my rearview mirror at the hound in the back seat. "It's going to be all right. For all three of us."

CHAPTER SEVEN

It *was* all right too, for over a year, then Grandma Rose's heart ticked its final beat, and with her went my last remaining tie to my mother.

I buried my grandmother's ashes in my grandfather's grave, as I had buried my dad's ashes in my mom's. They were all there together at the same cemetery for me to talk to when I felt the need.

But, not really.

There was a time when I believed Los Angeles was my forever home–that with my history there and all Southern California had to offer, it was the perfect place for me.

But, that was no longer true.

My doubt had finally coalesced into conviction. I knew I was not living the life I was meant to live, that there was some divine path I was meant to follow, and I would never find it if I remained rooted in L.A.

Riding home from work one evening, thinking about nothing in particular, out of the corner of my eye, I caught a glimpse of a house. The lights were just beginning to warm the windows. The people inside had yet to seal out the night.

A movement across the glass caused me to ease up on the gas. I stared transfixed by the come-together-dance taking place inside. A dog barked. A child shouted. A screen door slammed. Blurred waves twisted into focus behind the glass. Heads bent together, moved apart then disappeared into the back of the house. A round figure filled the window, reached up and dropped a curtain on the scene.

And there I was, left feeling like there was no place for me at their table. I turned my eyes to the rearview mirror and caught the headlights stacked up behind me. I accelerated, but then a hand reached into my heart and tugged hard. I slowed up one last time and glanced back over my shoulder, but that string of headlights had lost its patience. Two short honks forced my foot down on the accelerator and I disappeared back into my world.

A world that no longer expanded my view or my soul.

To be sure, that house and that family would not have challenged me either. I was drawn to it because it was safe. Too safe. But, there had to be a place for me at a table–somewhere–and I needed to find it. And, the search needed to start right then.

CHAPTER EIGHT

Sitting on our couch waiting for Harry to come home, I thought I might be sick. My stomach was in knots and my heart was so tight I was getting light headed. I had to pull it together. I was determined to break up with Harry *that day*. I had started to several times in the past few weeks, but was too chicken.

He was such a good guy. Kind. Easy-going. He saw me through the last of the Bobbi Jo years and my father's death. He had been helpful with Grandma Rose. He put up with my moodiness and my occasional insanity. He even accepted Mr. Bumbles–that's what I named the hound. And, Harry had been tolerating Alice's snooty ways for years.

I looked over at Alice, who was curled up next to me, and Mr. B, who was plopped down by the front door. "I'm doing it again, kids, talking myself out of leaving Harry." Neither one of them stirred.

My wishy-washy behavior had to stop. For as many good reasons as there were *not* to leave Harry, I had to anyway. Period. I loved him, but I wasn't *in love* with him, or the idea of us spending the rest of our lives together in Los Angeles.

I certainly wasn't doing him any kindness by staying with him when I felt that way. I needed to get a spine, be honest, and face the fallout.

Hearing footsteps outside the door, I took three deep breaths and told the muscles in my face and hands to relax.

Those muscles must not have cooperated, for the minute Harry saw me, the look on his own face indicated he knew something was up.

"Hey, Harry, how was your day?" I asked, in an effort to ease into the conversation. Like that was going to work. "It's hot out there. Can I grab a beer for you?"

"No, I'm good." He set the canvas bag he took to work down on the table next to the door.

"Water?"

"No." He wiped his forehead with the back of his arm. "What's up?"

"Would you sit down here?" I leaned over, picked up Alice's limp body and set her down on the floor. Then I patted the cushion that Alice had vacated.

"So?" he said, after he settled into the couch.

"So," I sighed. I was having a hard time getting the first words out, even though I had gone over them in my head. "This isn't working, Harry." Not the most sensitive way to begin a breakup, but with my pulse pounding in my temples it was the best I could come up with.

"What are you talking about?"

"You, me, this." I held my arm out to the apartment.

"What do mean? It's been working for five years."

"No. It really hasn't."

"You're just in a funk, Syd. Everybody gets that way. Your job's been bugging you. We haven't been on a vacation in a long time. But, that doesn't mean *we're* not working. We get along great. We have a lot of fun. We're good."

"Yes, but ..."

"It's just a rough patch, Syd. That's all." He cut me off.

"No, Harry. It's more than that. I ..."

"You just need to get away." Again, he cut me off. "A little change of scenery. While I was waiting to get my haircut the other day, I was reading about this retreat in Mexico, just over the border southeast of San Diego. Sounds like a good spot to recharge. We could go there. Maybe get some friends to come along."

"No, Harry! I don't need to go to Mexico, not with you, not with friends!" Oh boy. That was mean. My chest heavy with the hurt I knew I was going to inflict on him, I reached for both of his hands and held them in mine as I stared into his eyes, doing my best to keep mine dry. "Harry, a trip to Mexico is not going to fix anything. Let me ask you something." I shifted so that I was facing him straight on, our knees touching. "Where do you see us in five years?"

"Well, I figure by then maybe we'll be in a house."

"And?"

"And, we'll be better off in the money department, maybe you'll be doing that writing you're always taking about."

"But us, Harry. What about us?"

Harry hesitated, then understanding flickered in his eyes. "Oh, so marriage, that's what this is about! Because, you know, we haven't talked about it much, but we can if it's bothering you."

"No! It's not about marriage, Harry." He really wasn't getting it. "Not specifically. But, since you brought it up, why do you think we haven't talked about it much?"

"I don't know." He pulled his hands from mine and leaned back against the couch. "That sounds like one of those questions that no matter what I say, I'm wrong."

"Okay. Then I'll answer for us. We don't talk about marriage, because neither one of us is totally committed to this relationship. If we were, if we were crazy in love, if we were in this for eternity, we would already *be* married."

"Where did *that* come from? How many times have you told me that you don't believe in fairy tales? You don't even like romantic comedies."

"I know. I know. You're right. I don't believe in fairy tales, but there has to be more than this." I held my hands out, palms up. "Excitement, fire, purpose. And, it's not just about us; it's about our lives. Are you content to just hum along in neutral? Don't you want more? Don't you at least want to discover if there's someone or something out there that could make you crazy with passion?"

"Passion doesn't last."

"Maybe not. I don't know. But, I'd like to find out."

"So." Harry rubbed his jaw with his knuckles. "You want to leave me to go *find yourself*."

That last bit sounded as sarcastic as I had ever heard Harry. He wasn't the cynical type. But, he was hurt. Who could blame him? It wasn't like I had given him a lot of warning. Running out of steam, I sighed deeply and interlaced my fingers. "It probably makes no sense to you, but yeah, I do want to find myself, or at least find out what life is like beyond Southern California, and what *I'm like* someplace else."

"So, you're moving? Out of state?" Harry frowned. "When did you decide all this?"

"I've been thinking about it for awhile."

"Thanks for letting me know." Harry started to stand up.

"Wait, Harry." I put my hand around his forearm. "Would you sit for a minute? Let me explain." When he sat back down, his back stiff, I continued, "I've been wanting to tell you. It's just that I care about you so much. I don't want to hurt you. You're my best friend." My eyes started to well up. "But, I have to do this, Harry." My voice caught in my throat. "When I saw the box from my childhood, it did something to me. I mean, it made me feel like my life is so small, like if there was such a thing as reincarnation, this lifetime for me is a pass. I have contributed nothing." The tears started flowing down my cheeks.

"We don't have to cure cancer, Syd, for our lives to count." He perched on the edge of the couch like he was going to get up at any second.

"I know. I'm not looking to do something *that* big. But, I need to listen to my intuition. If I don't, I'll have regrets. I'll grow to resent you. I know it. I can't do that to you, or me."

"You sound like your mind's made up. Is it another man?" He stared hard at me.

"No. God, no, Harry. You know me better than that."

"Do I? Maybe not. I didn't see *this* coming."

"I hadn't seemed different to you lately?"

"Syd, you seem different to me every day. You've got a volatile personality. So, where are you going to *find yourself?* If you've been thinking about it for so long, you must know."

"New York."

"New York? That's a leap."

"Yeah, well, the thought of living in Manhattan has always intrigued me, and I should be able to get editing work there. I told you that my dad's brother, George, died. His memorial service is coming up on Saturday in Glendale, and it got me thinking maybe some of my dad's family from New York might be there. It would give me a chance to ask them about housing, things like that."

"You really *had* thought this through." He started to stand again, and this time I didn't stop him. "You might have let me in on it."

"I know. I'm sorry." I looked up at him, my vision blurred by my tears.

"You hammered the last nail on the coffin without ever even giving me a chance to talk it out with you, Syd." The anger rose in his voice. "You made up your mind, and that was it."

"I know." I was unable to meet his eyes.

"It's a mistake." He turned away.

"Maybe, but I need the chance to find that out for myself. I don't want to spend the rest of my life wondering about what might have been." I stood up and gently placed my hand on his shoulder. "I don't want to leave it like this, Harry."

"Yeah well, how did you think it was going to end?" He turned to face me.

"I thought maybe we could still be friends, you know."

"You just dumped me, Syd. Don't you think it might be a little soon to ask for my friendship?"

"I'm sorry. You're right. But, would you at least think about it?" I touched my fingers to his arm.

Looking down at my hand, he didn't respond. He turned and walked out the door.

CHAPTER NINE

Harry didn't return to our apartment for more than two weeks, at least when I was there. It wasn't fair to him that he was the one who moved out. I hadn't asked him to. I left several messages on his cellphone telling him I would find someplace else to go until my move.

He finally showed up one evening as I was packing up a few things from the kitchen. I didn't need a whole lot because my plans to go to New York had solidified far more quickly than I anticipated. I was going to be traveling there, however, by a mode of transportation that up until my Uncle George's memorial service was totally unfamiliar to me. It was via his old motorhome.

Turns out, there was a private reading of the will at the end of the service, and Uncle George left me that motorhome. I really had no clue why, other than we were both rabid Dodger fans and we had been to a few games together. He also left me his Sandy Koufax bobblehead doll and a baseball cap, which I was far more enthusiastic about than the motorhome. At least until my cousin Ralph from New York made me an offer I couldn't refuse.

Ralph flew out for the service as I had hoped, and gave me an earful about the price of rentals in Manhattan. If what he said was true, there was no way I could afford to live there. However, there was his neighborhood in the Bronx, the place where he grew up and where he still lived. It would be a bit of a commute, but according to him, there were plenty of trains into Manhattan.

When I was told about my inheritance of the motorhome, Ralph was right there with his offer. He had always wanted a motorhome, and was willing to trade me a few months' rent in his basement in the Bronx for it, if I was willing to drive it out to him. So, it was set. I, Sydney Roberts, was officially starting my life over–a scary and exhilarating prospect.

I related all of that to Harry as he watched me move from cupboard to cupboard in the kitchen, with Mr. Bumbles at his feet.

"You're sure it's all right to take these plates and glasses," I asked as I set them into a box.

"That's fine." He reached down to scratch Mr. B behind the ears.

Our initial hello had been awkward, like we were strangers. Not enough time had passed for either one of us to be over the ache of the breakup, particularly Harry, but at least he had come to see me. It would have been horrible to leave L.A. without saying good-bye to him.

"Have you practiced driving the motorhome? They can be pretty difficult to maneuver."

"Yeah. In a high school parking lot. It was pretty ugly at first, but I got the hang of it. Mostly." I smiled.

"Good to know." He smiled back.

What a relief seeing that smile was to me. It gave me the sense that there was at least an opening for us to remain friends. It wasn't fair to him, I know, but I needed an anchor back home as I set out on my journey. I said I wanted a challenge, but the thought of taking it on with zero contact with my past was a lot to ask of the new me.

"Do you have a triple A card?" he asked.

"Yeah."

"Good." He nodded. "You should probably check in every once in awhile, you know, with your driving solo and all, so we know that you haven't gotten lost in the middle of God knows where."

"I'll have Mr. Bumbles and Alice." I smiled.

"Oh yeah, well, Mr. B does have a good sense of direction."

"True."

Harry was quiet while I continued to add a few kitchen tools to my box.

"Hey, Harry," I said, hanging on to the edge of an upper cabinet door, "I really am sorry, you know."

"I know."

"Okay." I nodded. "Good."

When I finished packing, I showed Harry around the motorhome then asked if he wanted to take a walk on the beach.

He declined.

I got it.

But, when we parted, he reminded me to keep in touch.

There was that.

I did end up taking that last walk on the beach, with Mr. Bumbles by my side.

Kicking off my shoes, I curled my toes around the warm sand, imprinting the sensation into my memory. I had chosen to leave Southern California, but there were still many things I was going to miss.

Sitting down and crossing my legs, I put my arm around Mr. B's neck. The two of us stayed like that for a long time, watching the sun dip into the sea and the phosphorescent light dance across the flaming horizon.

Silently, I said good-bye to my home.

And, hello to my new life. I'd be kidding myself to say I didn't have my doubts. But, I was hopeful.

All I needed was faith, and trust, and a little pixie dust.

Keep reading for a sample from the next book
in the Sydney Roberts Series

FINDING HARMONY

And find out what
mysteries, romance, and misadventures await

Kicking a tumbleweed the size of a Volkswagen beetle aside, I cupped my hand over my eyes to block the intense afternoon sun and searched the road in both directions for any sign of life. Two days into my self-imposed journey of discovery and I didn't have a clue where I was. I was soon to discover, however, that it was not the Promised Land.

It had been such a dramatic departure too ... epic. Selling off most of my worldly goods, I packed up my Basset Hound and black and white cat and said a tearful but resolute good-bye to my ex. Hopping into my–well, not exactly *my*–motorhome, I set my compass for New York. It was time to forge a new life for my faithful companions and myself.

There I was, stranded on what must be the least traveled road in America, with no idea why the blue whale of the vehicle kingdom would sputter, clank, and refuse to go another mile. The motorhome was not my ideal choice of a medium from which to divine a new life, but it had given me the impetus to do so.

When I received the news that my part of my Uncle George's estate was his beloved motorhome, I was touched by the thought, but far from thrilled by the gift. My cousin Ralph, who had come out for the memorial service from New York, offered to trade me a few months in his basement apartment in the Bronx for it. By then I had already made up my mind to move from L.A., and the Northeast seemed like a good choice–plenty of culture and a lot of opportunity for work as an editor.

The only catch was that I would have to deliver the motorhome to Ralph. He couldn't miss any more work. I had always wanted to do the *Travels with Charlie* thing, so why not?

Day one had gone great too–L.A. to Vegas without a hitch–unless you consider the few tree branches I took out while learning to maneuver down side streets. Mr. Bumbles, that's my sad-eyed hound, and Alice, my saggy-bellied cat, and I thoroughly enjoyed our first evening cozied up in a casino parking lot under the neon glow of the Strip.

Day two had also begun well, with the three of us humming north on Interstate 15, and enjoying the air-conditioning fan ruffling my hair, Alice's fur, and Mr. Bumbles' ears. It would have been much more poetic if the wind had been doing the ruffling, but late August is not exactly a window-down time of the year in the Nevada desert.

Midday was spent at a quaint little park in St. George, Utah, after a short stop at a local supermarket where I added to my already well-stocked larder. When he glanced through the motorhome's cupboards, Harry, my ex, suggested that I had laid in enough food to supply a small scout troop for a year. But you can never have too many Fritos, *really*, even Alice likes them.

The source of my current predicament can be traced to that park in St. George, for it was there I met a little man with a very little Chihuahua, who insisted I take a detour to Zion National Park. He assured me that it would not be far out of my way, that there would be plenty of other people at the campground, and that its beauty would take my breath away. All I had to do was follow the scenic route out of town and I would be there in less than an hour.

Two hours later, the dust filling my lungs took my breath away all right. After one more glance in each direction, I decided help was not coming to find me, so I was going to have to find it.

Stepping back into the motorhome, I hooked Mr. Bumbles' leash to his collar and cast a glance at Alice, who was curled up in the driver's seat. She tends to take advantage of any opportunity to show who's really in charge. I debated whether to take her along, but decided it was impossible. There was no way that cat was going to stay in my arms for a minute, let alone all the way to the row of buildings I had noticed in the distance quite a ways back.

After cracking two windows, grabbing my purse and water, then locking all the doors, Mr. Bumbles and I headed out along the red silt strip next to the road. We had gone quite a distance, but progress was slow due to Mr. Bumbles' proclivity for inspecting every bush and anointing it with his personal holy water. Suddenly, he made a low woof, jerked at his leash, and took off after a cottontail rabbit that we scared up.

There was absolutely no way Mr. B was going to catch that thing, but his hound nose told him otherwise, and at sixty-five pounds, when the dog makes up his mind, there's no changing it. My only choice was to hang on until his legs or desire gave out. And hang on I did, until my right foot came into contact with a particularly low shrub and I took an ungainly swan dive into the dirt.

Before lifting my head, I did a mental damage assessment. Judging from the way my hands and knees were burning, they were obviously well scraped, and I was pretty sure the warm trickle down my left leg must be blood. I had a piercing pain in my right ankle, and as I ran my tongue around my mouth I realized that one of those bits of grit that I tasted was actually a tiny chunk of my left front tooth.

Moaning, I carefully rolled over and sat up. Yep, my shin was definitely bleeding, my ankle was definitely sprained, my tooth was definitely chipped, and I was definitely in deep shit.

Swiveling my head, I spied my purse a few feet away, the contents scattered. I noticed that the water bottle was missing just about the same time I felt a lump under my left rear cheek—one of the two I'm always promising to trim and tighten—in my dreams. Dragging the split plastic container out, I watched in morbid fascination as the last drop of water plopped to the red earth, leaving a nice little crimson puddle. Jeez, could things get any worse?

My hopes lifted as I noticed my cellphone sticking out from under a nearby bush. Dragging it toward me with my good left heel, I grabbed it, turned it on and held my breath as I waited for an indication that I was within range of a cell. Nope. No service. God knows why I thought the signal would be any better there than back at the motorhome. Useless piece of shit! I started to launch my phone to the heavens, then thought the better of it. After all, I wasn't going to be stuck in that little corner of Hell forever.

Or, was I?

Scanning the horizon, I began to worry about Mr. Bumbles. He had been gone for several minutes and I could no longer hear his baying. My only hope was that his loyalty and his nose would guide him back to me. In any event, I couldn't just sit there and wait for him. I was already very thirsty and I had no desire to spend the night with whatever critters lurked nearby. I prefer to keep the spooky monsters of the animal kingdom at a safe distance behind the glass of my television set.

Standing up, I tried putting a little weight on my bad ankle. Not so good, but it had to do. Moving slowly, I gathered up my belongings and was doing a slow 360 when I spotted the outline of the buildings that we had passed. They were still pretty far away, but if I continued across the desert in the direction that Mr. Bumbles had dragged me, it would certainly be a lot shorter than re-tracing my route back out to the road and the motorhome.

After what seemed like hours, but by my watch was thirty minutes, I was standing on a decomposed granite path leading to one of what looked like several dormitory buildings positioned in a regimentally straight row. The thing was, though, there was no evidence of a college in the immediate area, there was a very high chain-link fence around each building, and a very nasty looking dog roped to a cottonwood tree in this particular yard. I was pretty sure it wasn't a prison, but the whole place definitely had that narrow-windowed, cement-block jail motif–definitely not *Home and Garden Television* material.

I decided that rather than face the dog I would take my chances on the next dorm down. Had I seen myself in a mirror, I may have been able to attribute some of the treatment I received from the inhabitants of the strange enclave to sheer fright of the wild figure hobbling down their walk, in blood-streaked clothing and with auburn hair whipped into a *Bride of Frankenstein* frenzy.

As I approached the next gate, I noticed they too had a dog roped to a cottonwood. Mr. Bumbles. What a relief. When he saw me, he did the Bumbles happy dance, which involves much tail wagging, two full circles, and a series of low woofs. By the time he finished, his legs were hopelessly entangled in the rope, and without thinking I lifted the latch, pushed through the gate, and gimped over to him.

"Hey, boy." I stroked his dusty head. "Am I ever glad to see you."

Bending over and balancing on my good foot, I was untangling the rope when I noticed a flicker out of the corner of my eye. As I looked up, a flash of pink fabric disappeared around the corner of the building. I opened my mouth to call out, but my words were cut short by a deep male voice booming down on top of me, "You're trespassing!"

The little stability I was relying on to support me while helping Mr. B completely faltered as my heart rocketed to my throat and my shoulders jumped to my ears. I made my second unplanned dive of the day into Utah dirt, landing on my side, my bad ankle thrust in the air and pointing directly at a glowering face.

"Jesus, you frightened me. I didn't see you," I blurted out, the pulse in my ears so loud I felt like I was standing next to Niagara Falls.

"You *will not* take the Lord's name in vain!" The wrinkles between his world-record-length eyebrows drew into cavernous depths. "Now, get up!"

"Oh, uh, sorry." With shaking hands, I shifted my weight to my bottom, then reached down and cradled my ankle. "It's sprained." I lamely stared at his worn boots, afraid to look up. Mr. Bumbles had moved over next to me, so close the drops from his overhanging tongue were landing in my lap, but I didn't push him away. I needed somebody on my side.

Several seconds ticked by as the man continued to loom over me, apparently waiting for me to get up, which was just not going to happen, at least not without support. "I can't stand on it." I nodded my head at my ankle then finally dragged my eyes up to meet his chin. Making contact with his eyes was still asking a bit too much for my nerves.

Reaching down, he roughly pulled me to my feet and quickly drew back. Waving my arms like a tightrope walker, I finally regained a bit of my balance. When I finally found the courage to look over at him, he was not nearly as tall as he had seemed from my recumbent position. At five feet eleven, I am generally at or higher than eye level with many of the men I meet, and he was no exception. His lack of height, however, didn't do anything to detract from his menacing stance. With bulging crossed forearms and a head far too large for his body, he reminded me of Popeye with a Brutus attitude.

"Why are you here?" he asked, never taking his eyes off my face.

"My motorhome broke down and no cars came by, so I remembered seeing your buildings and was heading this direction." My nervousness shifted my speech into high gear.

"My dog took off after a rabbit, I tripped and sprained my ankle, then the dog got away. I spotted him here tied to your tree, so I let myself in," I finished, finally allowing myself to breathe.

"That's your dog?" he asked, staring at Mr. Bumbles.

"Yes." It came out more like a sigh.

"Angela!"

Whoa! There he went with the shouting again, and just when my heartbeat was beginning to slow down.

"Angela! I know you're back there. Get over here right now!"

I followed his gaze to the corner of the building where I thought I had seen movement. A thin, blonde-haired girl of about six slowly sidled around the building, head down.

"Hurry up!" he snapped.

She moved more quickly, but never raised her head. When she came within reach, he clamped his hand on her shoulder and drew her to stand directly in front of him.

"Where did this dog come from?" he asked.

"I found it," she murmured to the ground.

"Look at me when I talk to you," he snapped, lifting her chin with his index finger.

"I found it," she repeated softly, eyes glistening.

"Where?"

"The yard."

"Is that your answer?" He squeezed her chin.

After several moments, she closed her eyes and shook her head from side to side.

"Where, then?"

"Behind the house." She lifted her featherweight arm and pointed. "I thought he was lost."

"And does Mother Helen know you went out of the yard to get him?"

A trace of fear crossed her face then faded as she shook her head again.

"Then you need to march in the house and tell her what you have done."

"Yes, Father." The inflection and tempo of her words indicated they had been well practiced, but her eyes reflected more resignation than respect.

Turning her around by her shoulders, he gave her a soft shove in the direction of the large front door.

"Thanks for finding Mr. Bumbles for me," I called after her.

Glancing back over her shoulder, she mouthed the words, Mr. Bumbles, but didn't look at me or acknowledge what I had said.

"You have to leave." Mr. Congeniality untied the rope from Mr. Bumbles' leash and started to wind it around his hand.

"And exactly how do you expect me to do that?"

"That's really not my concern, now is it." He tucked the last of the rope into his palm and made a fist.

I stared at his balled hand. What was he planning to do, knock me out? "Look at me, Mister." I threw my arms out and teetered precariously on my good foot. "I'm not going anywhere without some help."

With blazing eyes, he surveyed me from head to foot then stared off into the distance, obviously trying to decide what to do. Finally, he grouched, "Wait here," and strode toward the door.

I looked down at Mr. Bumbles, who had been patiently watching the scene from his favorite position–seated, then bent over and picked up the end of his leash. "This is one fine mess we've gotten ourselves into, boy." I ran my thumb over the knot on the top of his head. He commiserated by raising an eyebrow.

After several minutes of staring at the front door, trying to determine if I had been abandoned, it finally opened and a woman who looked like the poster child for *Prairie Home Companion* walked down the steps carrying a white plastic chair. As she came closer I realized I had highly overestimated her age. She couldn't have been more than fifteen. Fifteen? And very pregnant. Is this a home for unwed mothers, I wondered, looking past her at the gray facade? Do they even have those anymore? But then, what about Mr. Congeniality and the little girl? None of it was adding up.

Averting her eyes, she set the chair down next to me. She lost her struggle with her curiosity, however, as she stole a peek at me under her dark lashes. Her face immediately reddened when I caught her eye, and she started to rush off, her long brown braid thumping her back. "Wait, please," I called after her. "I need ice for my ankle, and some water." The desperation in my voice must have been convincing because she stopped and turned around. "I'm totally dehydrated and Mr. Bumbles is too."

"Mr. Bumbles?" She frowned.

"My dog." I nodded at him.

"Oh." The beginning of a smile crept into her eyes and mouth as she looked at him, but quickly vanished.

"Please?"

"All right." She disappeared back into the house.

I guided myself into the chair, placing my right leg straight out in front of me. Mr. Bumbles plopped down beside me. After a few minutes, my Nightingale in calico returned with a plastic bag of ice and a cup of water for me, and a stainless steel bowl of water for Mr. B. Again, she turned to hurry off after making her delivery, but I gently placed my fingers on her forearm.

Stiffening like a plaster cast, she hesitated. I seized the moment. "Please don't rush away." I lightly pressed my fingers into her arm. "I really need to know what's going on."

"What do you mean?" She jerked her arm away from my hand, her voice a mixture of suspicion and fear.

My radar was buzzing big time. What the hell kind of place is this? Resisting the urge to shout that very question to the sky, knowing that she'd bolt, I calmly explained, "I need to know if your father is going to help me."

"Husband."

The cup of water was halfway to my lips when her answer sunk in. I dropped the cup back down. The water could wait. "Husband." It was a statement, not a question.

"Yes."

Scanning her face, I tried to assess her feelings about mothering the child of a man I estimated to be at least three times her age, but it revealed nothing. I was impressed. She had trained herself well.

"Well then, do you happen to know if your *husband* is going to help me?" I allowed myself two long draws of water as I waited for her answer.

"I am sure that he will. He is a benevolent man."

"That's comforting. He sounds like a real treasure," I said, far more sarcastically than I had intended. Her eyes widened. I quickly changed the subject. "What's your name?"

She set her jaw as if she was willing herself not to speak, and finally said, "Ruthie."

"Ruthie. Very pretty. I'm Sydney." I extended my hand, but she made no move to take it. Instead she looked over at the house.

"I have to help with dinner."

"Okay, Ruthie." I gave up, sensing that keeping her there was going to be next to impossible anyway. "You go. Thanks for the water and ice, and best wishes on that baby." I lifted my cup in a mock toast.

Her face reddened, much deeper this time. "Oh." She instinctively set her hand on her tight round belly. "Thanks."

"You might throw a little water our way if we're still sitting here in the morning." I smiled.

The beginnings of her own smile appeared again, but this time only reached as far as her eyes before another female voice called sharply from the door, "Ruthie!" like a mother to the fifteen-year-old child that she was. I was only able to catch a glimpse of a long brown and silver braid as the two of them faded into the dusk of the house.

I had just managed to figure out the best way to keep ice on my ankle when Mr. Congeniality was back towering over me.

"I called the town mechanic. He'll be here after he closes his shop." He put his hand on the back of my chair, brushing my shoulder.

Startled, I leaned forward, wondering what he was doing.

"You can wait on the road beyond the gate." He tipped the chair forward, barely giving me a chance to remove the ice from my ankle and get my feet set.

"That's really generous of you." Clenching my jaw, I adjusted my purse over my shoulder and held Mr. Bumble's leash in one hand and the ice in the other.

Mr. Congeniality's response was to march deliberately to the gate, unlatch it, walk fifty paces down the road, set the chair down, and return just in time to pass me as I was hobbling slowly through the gate like an octogenarian on a field trip.

"Benevolent," I said to the air as I heard him shut the door to the house behind me.